1395

Birthday Poems

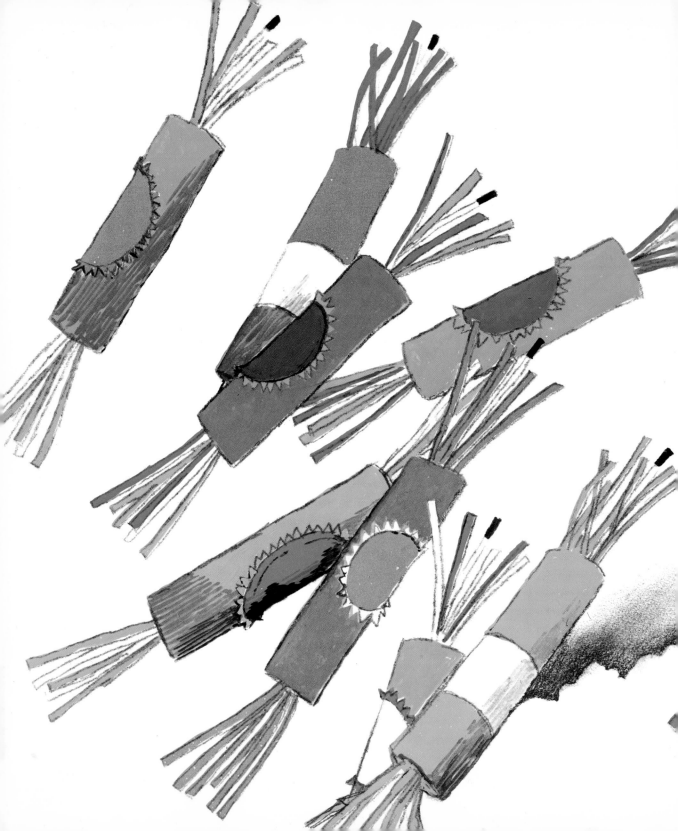

Birthday Poems

Myra Cohn Livingston

illustrated by
Margot Tomes

Holiday House/New York

To THOMAS PERKINS

Text copyright © 1989 by Myra Cohn Livingston
Illustrations copyright © 1989 by Margot Tomes
All rights reserved
Printed in the United States of America
First Edition

Library of Congress Cataloging-in-Publication Data

Livingston, Myra Cohn.
Birthday poems / written by Myra Cohn Livingston ; illustrated
by Margot Tomes.— 1st ed.
p.   cm.
Summary: A collection of poems celebrating the many
aspects of birthdays.
ISBN 0-8234-0783-7
1. Birthdays—Juvenile literature.   2. Children's poetry.
American. [1. Birthdays—Poetry.   2. American poetry.]
I. Tomes, Margot, ill.   II. Title.
PS3562.I945B5   1989
811'.54—dc19   89-2114   CIP   AC

ISBN 0-8234-0783-7

CONTENTS

BEACH BIRTHDAYS

1)   At the beach
           on my birthday
           we built a sand castle.

           We watched
           while the waves
           swept our castle away,

           with its ramparts
           and bailey
           and turrets
           and drawbridge,

           And *I* was the King of the Castle that day!

2)   At the beach
           on my birthday
           we built a sand castle,

           with a drawbridge
           and forest
           and moat in between;

           a tower where we could look out on the ocean—

           I'll always remember
           the day I was queen!

TRAY

Of all the party games
we play
Ann's favorite is always *Tray*

when someone fills
a big tray up
with spoons or pencils, and a cup

and saucer, rubber bands
or string.
We have to look at everything

like dimes or stickers
or a key
and then remember what we see

when someone
covers up the tray;
so then we all take turns to say

what we remember.
Matt goes first.
Sarah's memory is worst.

Laura giggles,
and I try—
Chris gets mad enough to cry.

When we're finished
Ann just grins
because she always, *always* wins!

BIRTHDAY CAKE

Chocolate
or butter
or angel food cake—

    whatever you stir
    or whatever you bake,

    please put sugar icing on—
    swirly and thick—

    for a cake's
    not a cake
    without icing to lick!

BIRTHDAY CLOWN

A clown came to Pat's party.
    He did a lot of tricks.
He played a guessing game with us
    And guessed that Pat was six.

He made all kinds of magic
    Where things would disappear.
One time he looked around and found
    A dime behind Pat's ear.

He showed us how to tie balloons,
    One came out like a cat.
The best was like an elephant,
    Especially for Pat.

He gave out cards and said to call
    And say hello sometime.
A clown came to Pat's party.

I hope he comes to mine!

BIRTHDAY NIGHT

After my birthday
    I couldn't get sleepy.
    I wanted to stay up.
    I wanted to play
      with all of my presents
      and never get sleepy.

How *could* I sleep after
    my wonderful day?

11

DINOSAUR BIRTHDAY

All of us went for Jan's birthday
On the bus and past hundreds of stores
To a block where they have a museum
And a place where they keep dinosaurs.

All of us crossed with the green light
Past the traffic and people and shops
To the room where they have Brontosaurus,
Allosaurus and Triceratops.

All of us liked ceratopsians,
All of us loved stegosaurs,
All of us plan to spend birthdays
Visiting *more* dinosaurs!

BIRTHDAY SECRETS

1)   When my dog had a birthday
              he got a big bone.
For my dolls we served
              cookies and tea,
But I want a birthday
              with ice cream and cake
And a *whole bunch* of presents for *me!*

2)   When Joan had a birthday
             she only asked four,
Ann and Betty and Sue and Marie.
But I want to ask every friend
          that I know
Who will bring *lots of presents* for me!

3)   I know it is selfish,
I know it's not nice,
(I'm as greedy as greedy can be)
      But I hope everyone I've invited will come

      and bring *wonderful* presents for me!

PARTY DRESS / PARTY SHIRT

1)   My party dress
        had spots of pink
          before the ice cream came;

    But now the spots
        are pink and brown

        and chocolate is to blame!

2)   My party shirt
        was blue and white
          before the ice cream came;

    But now my shirt
        is chocolate too—

        and ice cream is to blame!

PINNING THE TAIL ON THE DONKEY

Pinning the tail
on
the
donkey

is a
game
that's
as fun
as can
be

except
for the time
Charlotte
got all mixed up

and started to pin it on *me!*

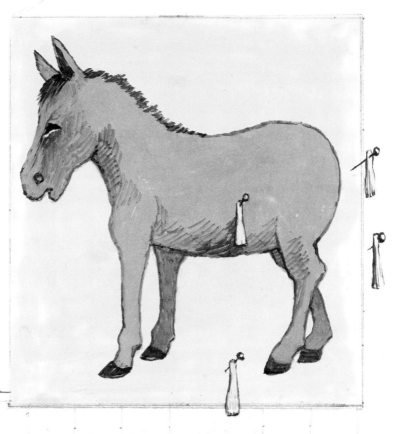

17

FUNNY GLASSES

When Hilary won
 she got the prize,
  some funny glasses for her eyes
 that made the world
  turn red and blue.

I wish *I'd* won.
I'd like some too.

FOUR

Our baby's *one*,
And Meg is *two*.
Elaine is nearly *three*.

But I'll be *four* next Saturday
And *four*'s the best to be!

FIVE

is old enough
to know
to get up early
and to go
and wake up everyone
to say

I'm finally *five years old* today!

19

SIX

One year we had a picnic.

One year a pony came.

One year there was a puppet show.

This year we have a game
       of playing Hot Potato
       and House
       and Pick-up-sticks.

This year's my favorite birthday.
This year I'm turning *six*!

SEVEN

ONE
    I don't remember

TWO
    I have forgot

THREE
    was swinging at the park

FOUR
    we swam a lot

FIVE
    we saw the circus

SIX
    was games to play
    but

SEVEN
    I'll remember
      because
        seven
          is
           today!

EIGHT

My birthday
comes so slowly,
I don't know how I'll wait

But watch out
for next Thursday
when I'll suddenly turn *eight*!

INVITATION

My birthday invitation
    has balloons
    of red and blue.

It says *come soon*
    and *please reply*,

My name is on it too.

It tells the place where we will meet
And shows the time and date.

So *please reply*
And say you'll *come*

    to help me celebrate!

MICHAEL'S BIRTHDAY

At Michael's party
   we hiked out
     along a nature trail.

Matthew saw a hill of ants.
Carter squished a snail.

Henry found a bunch of lizards
Basking in the sun.

Jim looked out for fossil rocks
And tracks where deer had run.

Dick and I picked lots of twigs
To make the fire start
So we could roast our hot dogs

And the food was the best part!

25

THE HAYRIDE

When Peter turned seven
    we went for a hayride,
    a wonderful hayride
    up over the hill.

We sang Happy Birthday
    and Peter threw haystraws
    on Heather and Tammy
    and Lindsey and Bill.

Everyone scrambled
    and everyone giggled
    when Lindsey and Tammy
    and Heather and Bill

Took Peter and gave him
    a real birthday spanking
    the minute we started
    to ride down the hill!

PARTY PRIZES

We wrapped a prize for every game
And on the package put the name.
But when we got to Blind Man's Bluff
And Evan won, that was enough
Because he'd won the Three-Legged Race,
So Ellie, who came second place,
Got Evan's prize and Tod got hers
And when we played Tag, Tod got first
So he gave his to Mary Lou,
And by the time the games were through
We found, to everyone's surprise,
That *everybody* won a prize!

PARTY FAVORS

Sally gave harmonicas.
Laura gave red balls.
Kristen gave toy watches
        and paper parasols.
Karen gave us tiny little padlocks
        with a key,

But I'll give red kazoos
            because
        kazoos are best for me!

PARTY TABLE

We have a paper tablecloth
   with dogs and dancing cats
   and paper plates
   and paper cups
   and matching paper hats
     and forks for eating up the cake
     and poppers
     and white spoons
     and whistles for the favors
     and a bunch of pink balloons,
       a plate with wrapped-up candy
       a dish with bubble gum

     and now the table's ready
     for my birthday guests to come!

PRESENTS

My friends all gave me presents.

I got a gyroscope,
    some bubble bath,
    a paddle ball,
    a singing jumping rope,
    some finger paints,
    some paper dolls,
    a magnifying glass,
    a Fuzzy Felt Safari game,
    a swan spun out of glass,
    a picture book,
    a Teddy bear,
    a pencil,
    and two banks,
    and stationery with my name
    to send my friends my thanks—

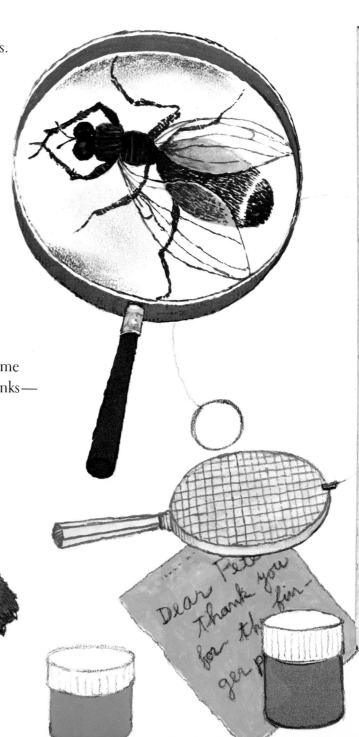

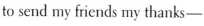

BICYCLE BIRTHDAY

This is my bicycle birthday,
    my bicycle shining and blue;
        I hope when you're having a birthday
            they'll give you a bicycle too,
                a bicycle sparkling and new,
                    (a tricycle simply won't do),
                        I hoped that my wish would come true—
                            I thought, but I didn't know who
                                would give me a bicycle. *You?*

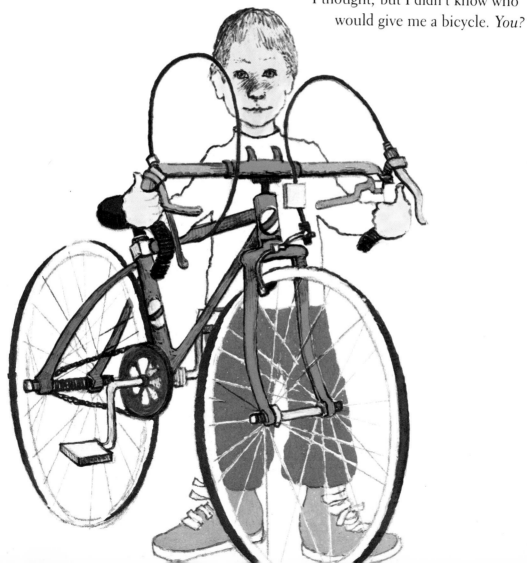

BIRTHDAY WISH

And after they have sung the song,
       the birthday song,
       the song I know,
The candles sparkle on the cake
And then I get to blow
       and blow—

I stand up
And I take a breath
And blow my way
Around the cake

And all my head is dancing with
The birthday wish I get to make!